The Rubber-Legged Ducky

John G. Keller ✒ Illustrated by Henry Cole

HARCOURT, INC.
ORLANDO   AUSTIN   NEW YORK   SAN DIEGO   LONDON

Requests for permission to make copies of any part of the work should be submitted online at
www.harcourt.com/contact or mailed to the following address:
Permissions Department, Harcourt, Inc., 6277 Sea Harbor Drive, Orlando, Florida 32887-6777.

www.HarcourtBooks.com

Library of Congress Cataloging-in-Publication Data
Keller, John G.
The rubber-legged ducky/John G. Keller; illustrated by Henry Cole.
p. cm.
Summary: A duckling with a rubber-band leg uses it to save the brood from a fox that is looking for supper.
[1. Ducks—Fiction. 2. Foxes—Fiction. 3. Rubber bands—Fiction. 4. Individuality—Fiction.]
I. Cole, Henry, 1955– ill. II. Title.
PZ7.K28134Rub 2008
[E]—dc22 2006102851
ISBN 978-0-15-205289-8

First edition
A C E G H F D B
Manufactured in China

The illustrations in this book were done in acrylic and ink
on Arches hot press watercolor paper.
The display and text type was set in Tweed.
Color separations by Colourscan Co. Pte. Ltd., Singapore
Manufactured by South China Printing Company, Ltd., China
Production supervision by Pascha Gerlinger
Designed by Kristine Brogno and Michele Wetherbee

In memory of John A. Keller,
who first told me about Five.—J. G. K.

To D. K. W.—H. C.

One sunny day while Mama Duck was in the farmyard, nibbling on weeds and chomping on bugs, she accidentally ate a rubber band.

Now, Mama Duck didn't think much about that rubber band. But the next time she hatched a brood, she noticed something strange. One, Two, Three, and Four said, "Quack, quack" as they tapped out of their shells. But Five did no such thing.

He cried, "Bing-boing!"

And when that fifth duckling followed his brothers
and sisters down to the pond for a first swim, he didn't
waddle. Five bounced—and more than just a little.

Mama's heart skipped a beat. She drew Five under her wing and said softly, "Five, listen to me. You are different from the others, but you are my special ducky, and that means you can do special, wonderful things."

Most of the other animals saw nothing special about Five.

"He bounces!" snickered the goat.

"He doesn't quack!" squealed the pigs.

"That duckling is bad news," muttered the rooster.

Mama Duck paid those animals no attention. Instead she gathered her ducklings about her. She told them about life on the farm. And she warned them about two things to watch out for: hawks and foxes—*especially* foxes. The ducklings all listened and nodded. Then they went about their business.

Five soon showed why he was special.

"I can't reach those berries," Two cried.

Five just bounced high on his rubber leg, grabbed the tallest branch, and held it down so Two could nibble the sweet fruit.

Every afternoon, Five let Three strum on his leg while they sang a duet.

"Thrum, thrum...
    bing-boing...quack!"

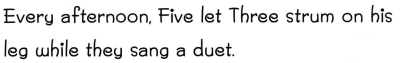

They thought they sounded great together.

And when he saw a bully piglet pick on Four, Five thought a minute.

Then he lassoed the piglet's nose with his rubber leg and wouldn't
let go until the bully squealed, "Sorry!"

Then one afternoon, while the farm animals drowsed in the sun, a gang of crows wheeled across the sky. "Fox! Fox in the neighborhood," they cawed. "Watch out!"

The animals quickly assembled.

"Don't worry," grunted the pigs. "We can smell a fox way off. Phew! Plenty of time to warn you."

"I'll butt him," bleated the goat.

"I'll crow my best to alert the farmer. That will solve the problem," bragged the rooster. Then he gave a great crow just to show off.

Five said nothing, but he had ideas of his own.

Sure enough, the very next night the fox came calling.
All the animals were sleeping—not an oink or crow was heard.

The moon shone on the fox's very white, very sharp teeth.
Yum, yum, he thought as he licked his lips, *I smell duckling*.

At that instant, Five opened his eyes.

"Bing-boing!" cried Five,
sounding the alarm. "Fox! Run, everyone!"
The chase was on.

Mama Duck led her
ducklings to the water.

Splash!

One, Two, Three, and Four
followed close behind.

Splash!...Splash...
splash...splash!

"Hurry, Five," they quacked. "RUN!"

But Five stayed right where he was.

"Hey, old Foxy Loxy," he teased, "you can't catch me."

The fox turned toward Five and opened up his great, big, gleaming jaws.

Boing! Five shot his rubber leg right into the fox's mouth!

The fox bit down, but Five was brave, so he didn't care. He just flapped his wings and paddled with his one leg as hard as he could. As he flapped and paddled, a wonderful thing happened. Five's rubber leg began to stretch... and stretch... and s-t-r-e-t-c-h until it could stretch no more.

Silly duckling, the fox thought, *now you will be my tasty supper.*
But oh, that fox was wrong.

Five folded his wings, stopped paddling—and then suddenly went zooming backward across the water.

BANG! He hit the astonished fox right square on the nose.

"BOING!" cried Five.

"EYOW!" yelped the fox, and when he opened his jaws,
Five jumped back into the water and swam to safety.

The sound of all that quacking, boinging, and yelping woke up
the farmer, and he ran to the pond and chased the fox away.

All the animals gathered around Five.

"You're brave," bleated the goat.

"Clever," oinked the pigs.

"Special," agreed the rooster. "Very special."

Pleased that his plan had worked so well, Five modestly nibbled some grass. There was a small silence. Then Mama Duck said, "Well, I think we've all had enough excitement for one evening.... It's time for a soothing swim and then back to sleep. Come along, children."

Mama Duck hopped into the pond. Then she and her five ducklings swam away—
quacking and bing-boinging into the moonlight.